SECOND EDITION

50

POWERFUL

WAYS TO

WIN NEW

CUSTOMERS

Fast, simple, inexpensive, profitable and proven ideas you can use starting today!

By
Paul R. Timm, Ph.D.

SECOND EDITION

50 POWERFUL WAYS TO WIN NEW CUSTOMERS

Fast, simple, inexpensive, profitable and proven ideas you can use starting today!

By
Paul R. Timm, Ph.D.

CAREER PRESS
3 Tice Road
P.O. Box 687
Franklin Lakes, NJ 07417
1-800-CAREER-1
201-848-0310 (NJ and outside U.S.)
FAX: 201-848-1727

50 POWERFUL WAYS TO WIN NEW CUSTOMERS, 2ND ED.
FAST, SIMPLE, INEXPENSIVE, PROFITABLE AND PROVEN IDEAS
YOU CAN USE STARTING TODAY!
ISBN 1-56414-307-4, $8.99
Cover design by Digital Perspectives
Printed in the U.S.A. by Book-mart Press

To order this title by mail, please include price as noted above, $2.50 handling per order, and $1.50 for each book ordered. Send to: Career Press, Inc., 3 Tice Road, P.O. Box 687, Franklin Lakes, NJ 07417.

Or call toll-free 1-800-CAREER-1 (in NJ and Canada: 201-848-0310) to order using VISA or MasterCard, or for further information on books from Career Press.

Library of Congress Cataloging-in-Publication Data
Timm, Paul R.
50 powerful ways to win new customers: fast, simple, inexpensive, profitable, and proven ideas you can use starting today! / by Paul R. Timm. --2nd ed.
p.   cm.
Based on: 50 ways to win new customers.
Includes index.
ISBN 1-56414-307-4
1. Small business--Management. 2. Advertising--Cost effectiveness.
3. Marketing--Cost effectiveness. 4. Customer services. I. Timm, Paul R. 50 ways to win new customers.
II. Title.
HD62.7.T5   1997
658.8--dc21   97-17751
                                                                    CIP

Dedication

I am constantly amazed at the examples of symbolism over substance in organizations. Every organization talks about the importance of customers, and many have slogans touting that "the customer is number one" or "the customer is always right." But how many translate these slogans and good intentions into practical, day-to-day actions that win customers for life? Not many.

That's the good news! Because people and companies that get serious about winning customers—who create an ongoing strategy for doing so—will reap huge rewards.

This book, and my earlier Career Press book, *50 Powerful Ideas You Can Use to Keep Your Customers,* are my contributions to the cause of more satisfying customer relationships and more successful businesses.

As you read this book, make it your goal to identify five or six ideas for immediate application. Then look for several more you can use next month, and so forth. Try new ideas and observe their results. By doing these things you will begin to harness the power of continuous quality improvement.

This book is dedicated to those who recognize that there is no traffic on the extra mile—and to those who are determined to run it.

Contents

Introduction   **9**

Part 1
Attract New Customers   **15**

Part 2
Motivate Customers   **55**

Part 3
Retain Current Customers   **65**

Part 4
Restore the Lost Customer   **97**

A Final Few Words   **117**

About the Author   **119**

Index   **121**

Introduction

Businesses fail for a number of reasons, but three kinds of customer-related issues account for most failures:

1. Not enough customers.
2. Not the right customers.
3. Not the right products for the company's customers.

Eighty percent of customer-related business failures arise from simply not having enough customers. Either the company fails to attract a sufficient customer base or it lets existing customers slip away.

Let's look at some typical examples of businesses that are failing. Although these illustrations are from retail or small businesses, the problems are equally applicable to larger and nonretailing businesses.

What's wrong with these pictures?

Jon and Marie Passive decided to start a business. They both loved reading, so a bookstore seemed natural. They contacted wholesalers, selected a product line they wanted to sell, and came up with a company name, *Verbose Books & Tapes*. They rented a store, put up an attractive sign, ran a few ads in the newspaper and sat back, expecting the customers to beat a path to their door for the best book and tape deals in town.

After a few months of sitting in their new store from 9 a.m. to 9 p.m., Jon and Marie realized that something just wasn't working quite the way they'd anticipated. They had very few customers.

❖ ❖ ❖ ❖ ❖

Sandra and Ralph went a slightly different route in their search for business success. They bought a *Fat Freddy's* hamburger restaurant franchise ("Home of the really big buns"). The home office gave them standardized training and lots of advice on how to make the restaurant profitable and keep costs down. But they didn't get much advice on how to compete with the *Wendel's Burger Hut* across the street. While *Wendel's* seemed to wallow in customers, Sandra's and Ralph's big buns went stale on the shelf.

❖ ❖ ❖ ❖ ❖

Lynn's problem was a little different. Her variety store did really well for the first six years until a giant chain *(Wally-World)* opened up nearby. *Wally-World* was famous for selling a huge variety of goods at extremely competitive prices. It had been so successful at putting competitors under that the business press had dubbed them "The merchant of death." How in the world can a small store like Lynn's compete with such a giant?

❖ ❖ ❖ ❖ ❖

Finally we have Tom's situation. He works as a sales representative for a well-known office products company. His sales, especially in computer software, are off substantially. Most customers complain about a down market, but he suspects they are buying elsewhere. Nobody wants to tell him directly, but they can get better service from his main competitor. And that's where they are going.

❖❖❖❖❖

While these examples are from retail or small businesses, this basic problem arises in all kinds of businesses. In fact, it is the single greatest business killer: the failure to *win* customers.

Don't just get them to consider doing business with you; don't just get them to buy once or twice; win them for the long run. That is the hallmark of any successful business or businessperson.

Apply the tips you'll learn in this book and you'll be light-years ahead of others in your ability to win customers. The process is simple, yet not easy. It can be applied in any organization or, for that matter, in any *kind* of relationship. The principles here can be used to strengthen marriages and families while also bolstering businesses. The techniques are the same. And your success will depend upon only four things:

1. Awareness of the techniques available.

2. Willingness to try some new ideas.

3. Attention to the "little things."

4. Consistent application.

In short, this book will show you how to increase your customer base and enjoy the highest possible profitability.

The bottom line of all these examples: Failure to win customers is the single greatest business killer. So how do we overcome this problem. I'm glad you asked. This is what this book is all about. Here you will find some specific, high-impact actions you can take to win customers—loyal repeat customers.

Winning customers is a two-step dance

What do I mean by "winning" a customer? Simply put, winning is a two step dance.

1. Attract and motivate customers to your products or services.

2. Retain (and, if necessary, restore) customers.

Many new businesses scramble to get new customers in the door but fail to follow through with step two. The loyal customer who does repeat business and recommends us to others is the one who makes us the greatest profit. To entice someone to try us without doing all that we can to establish customer loyalty is exceptionally shortsighted. So, when it comes to the dance of *winning* customers, both steps are equally important.

The chart below shows an overview of four action categories that will determine whether you win your customers. The left column focuses on getting people to take the first step—trying your products or services. The right column focuses on the second step in the dance—hanging on to the customer's business.

The Four Action Categories for Winning Customers

Step 1 Get Customers To Try You	Step 2 Build Customer Loyalty
ATTRACT • Project your attitude. • Advertise. • Network.	**RETAIN** • Exceed expectations. • Improve constantly.
MOTIVATE • Offer incentives. • Incite to action.	**RESTORE** • Value "lost" customers. • Win them back.

Dance step 1

We can't demonstrate our commitment to a long-term customer relationship unless people give us a try. This happens when we attract and motivate people. Attraction happens when we project an attitude that causes customers to be interested in us and our business. We can also trumpet our company's virtues so that people will think of us when a need for our product arises. This can be done through advertising, although the effectiveness of standard advertising is often disappointing. Attraction also happens through networking: people spreading the word among their friends or associates. When our customers tell others about us, word of mouth exposure happens, for better or worse. If our customer likes what we do, word of mouth attraction can be the most powerful form of advertising.

Dance step 2

Once people agree to try us, we have a valuable opportunity to exceed their expectations.

The power of exceeded expectations is only now being fully understood. People's buying decisions are largely emotional and emotions are based on perceptions. If people perceive that they are getting more from your company than they expected, they almost always feel a sense of commitment to be a good customer. Occasionally, of course, things go wrong and a customer has a bad experience. Should we just write off that customer and go back to step one to win another customer? Usually, no. Recovering "lost" customers pays big dividends. This book will give you many specific tips for retaining customers, thus fulfilling the second step in the process of winning.

Part 1

Attract New Customers

Three kinds of action will attract customers and entice them to try the products or services of your business or organization:

1. Project positive and inviting attitudes.

2. Network to use the power of word of mouth.

3. Advertise effectively and creatively.

1.
Start with an attitude of gratitude.

Be thankful for customers. Customers are very special people. Of all the billions of people on this planet, only a tiny fraction will choose to do business with you. Treat your customers like the golden resources they are. Do you always do that?

If you or your employees have ever thought, "This would be such a great job if it weren't for the customers," you run a real risk of projecting that attitude. People have a sixth sense. If you see them as an inconvenience or burden, they'll sense it.

Nobody has to do business with you; they choose to. In making that choice, they are doing you a service. Sure, you provide them with important goods and services that meet their needs, but they still choose you. Be appreciative.

Also be appreciative that we work in a free economy where we are free to compete for the approval of customers. Make the process of winning customers a lifelong hobby; make it fun.

Commit, starting today, to appreciate your customers and make that attitude show.

2.
DON'T TRY TO TEACH A PIG TO DANCE.

If you don't have that attitude of gratitude, or if you simply don't like people, throw this book away. You'll never win or keep customers. It's okay. Just accept yourself for what you are and go into a job that doesn't require contact with others (if you can find one).

Likewise, when you hire employees, be sure they like people. Watch the ways they interact with all kinds of people. Be sure you are careful in selecting who will represent your company. Don't take the hiring process lightly. Hiring involves a long-term commitment and if your employees fall short in customer service, they'll do you more harm than good.

Anyone can fake behaviors for a while, but if you observe your prospective employees carefully, you'll see how well they hold their positive attitude. They'll probably work for you for a long time, so be sure you hire correctly in the first place.

I recall interviewing for a job as a sales representative for Xerox years ago. Each time I thought they had decided to hire me, I learned that someone else wanted to do another interview. This went on for weeks and I was eager to get on with the job. Frankly, I was getting frustrated and was tempted to tell them to fish or cut bait. I needed a decision.

Now I see what they were doing. They were testing my frustration level. They wanted to see how I'd act when a customer would waffle on a buying decision.

3.
Do an organizational reality check.

Most companies say that the customer is number one. Sure, sure. A bank in my town came up with the clever slogan, "Currently Giving 110%" to convey their commitment to service. Unfortunately, the slogan was not accompanied with any actions. No employees received special service training, nothing special was planned other than posting the slogan on billboards around town. The result: I asked a teller at the bank what the slogan meant. Her response, "Beats me. I just read it on the billboard on the way to work today."

A slogan can never substitute for a strategy. Strategies involve implementation of actions and behaviors while empty slogans do not.

So, before you start believing your own press clippings (or advertisements), come up with answers to these *potentially disquieting questions* about customer service in your organization that I ask my clients.

Does your company...

1. Talk about customer service but pay front-line people a low, flat wage?

2. Offer little or no ongoing training in the basics of good service for customer contact people?

3. Offer no special incentives for taking care of the customer?

4. Punish or reprimand an employee's poor customer service but take good service for granted?

5. Place greater emphasis on winning new customers than retaining ones you already have?

6. Fail to reward or recognize employees who support contact people's efforts to serve customers?

7. Hold "be nice to the customer" programs or campaigns that last for a few weeks or months but are soon forgotten?

8. Have top managers who rarely, if ever, face live customers or devote time to listening to customers and helping them solve problems?

9. Make no effort to measure service quality as perceived by customers?

10. Make no attempt to hold managers at all levels accountable for the service level?

An affirmative answer to any of these questions can be a red flag to you. While all organizations talk about customer satisfaction, many unwittingly discourage it by doing the things described above. Where does your organization stand?

4.
Judge not, assume the best.

Sales trainer Joe Girard (who modestly bills himself "the world's greatest salesman") talks about the importance of having a positive attitude toward all people. Don't judge them or put them into some category. Assume they are and will continue to be your customers. Joe puts it this way:

> *However I feel about myself or whoever I'm with, I don't let my feelings get in the way. This (selling) is a business we're in, an important profession. And those people, those prospects, those customers are the most important thing in the world to us, to each of us. They aren't interruptions or pains in the ass. They are what we live on. And if we don't realize that, as a hard business fact, then we don't know what we are doing. I'm not talking about some of them or most of them. I'm talking about all of them.* (Joe Girard, *How to Sell Anything to Anybody,* New York: Simon and Schuster, 1977, p. 47.)

Sales trainers teach people to be "assumptive." *Assume* that a person is going to buy, and treat him or her accordingly. The power of assumption really works. It's like positive thinking. It somehow projects to the customer and becomes a self-fulfilling prophecy.

J. D. Salinger said, "I *am* a kind of paranoid in reverse. I suspect people of plotting to make me happy." With an attitude like that, we'd look forward to every meeting with every customer.

Of course, we quickly learn that some customers do not seem to be plotting to make us happy. Most are very pleasant. Some are unusual. A few are downright difficult. Occasionally you face the "Customer from Hell."

Every person is different; each has a unique personality. But the *kind* of people who tend to bug us the most are the ones who *are not like us.* Accept this diversity and learn to enjoy it. Know that people's needs are basically the *same* at some level and that *treating them like guests* will create the most goodwill and a powerful basis for good customer relations.

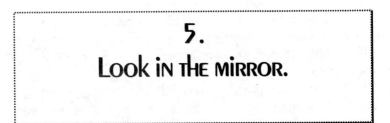

5.
Look in the mirror.

From the moment we meet people, we begin to size them up. What we decide about their trustworthiness and ability is largely a factor of first impressions. And as the old saying goes, you only get one chance to make that first impression.

An owner of an auto repair shop tried an experiment. He paid each of his repair people on commission for the amount of repair work they did. He invited the mechanics to volunteer to change their dress and grooming. Several agreed to cut their hair, shave daily and wear clean uniforms. Those who did created far more repeat business than the others. The customers would ask for the better dressed mechanics, and those who chose to dress and groom themselves in the "old way" found they were getting less work.

The key word in dress and grooming is *appropriate*. Salespeople in a surf shop would look foolish in three-piece suits; an undertaker would look ludicrous in a Hawaiian sport shirt.

The importance of dress explains why some organizations provide uniforms. It used to be more widespread. Nurses, delivery people and bank employees were given attractive full or partial uniforms that projected professionalism. Many employees appreciated this. It saved them money on a work wardrobe. Perhaps your company could benefit from such a practice. It can certainly set an organization apart from its competition.

6.
Check the appearance of your work area.

"A cluttered desk is the sign of a cluttered mind," says the desk plaque. Likewise, a cluttered business or work area conveys a sense of disorganization and low professionalism.

Look around you and see what your customer sees. Is merchandise displayed attractively? Is the place clean and tidy? Does the work space look organized and efficient?

Granted, some people work very well in a mass of clutter. I know of a plumbing supply store that looks like a tornado casualty, yet the old-timer who runs the place can find anything he needs. I also know more then a few professors who seem to thrive amongst an avalanche of paper. But these are rare birds.

If you find yourself spending too much work time looking for things or helping customers find misplaced items, it's time to de-junk.

Cleaning out the clutter can be cathartic. It feels good. Every six months or so I do a thorough de-junking of my office and files. Most of the stuff people keep in files never gets looked at again. Keep key records or materials required by law, but take a hard look at all the other stuff. Save items electronically and back up your computer files regularly, but don't keep a paper copy too!

7.

TEACH PROSPECTIVE CUSTOMERS.

An auto repair shop offers a series of seminars on how cars work. These sessions are free and open to the public. Each week, people can choose the minicourse they'd like to attend. A mechanic explains brakes, suspension systems, mufflers and pollution controls, and other aspects of how cars work. After the classes, people are invited for coffee and donuts.

This service helps potential customers feel comfortable around the business and gets them acquainted with the employees.

Many products and services we sell today require some customer education. One argument for the success of network marketing (also called multilevel marketing or direct sales) is that it involves neighbors selling products and services to neighbors. It is very personalized, thus allowing more teaching opportunities.

A striking example of the effectiveness of the teaching element in marketing arises from the process of telephone deregulation over the past decade. Prior to 1986, all long distance telephone service in the United States was handled by AT&T. Changes in the laws gave customers the opportunity to choose another long-distance carrier if they wished. Many people were confused by this. Nevertheless, AT&T eventually lost 50 percent of that market. And of the 50 percent that was lost, 30 percent was taken by network marketing.

When the customer is uncertain, personalized, face-to-face selling, such as that done by multilevel sales organizations, can provide the education needed for the buyer to feel comfortable about a change in provider. Incidentally, this scenario is about to repeat as other public utilities (electric, gas, cable TV, etc.) are being deregulated. My guess is that network marketing will be a major force in teaching and selling customers on alternate sources of these products.

Other business people volunteer to come into schools, church groups or civic organizations to teach about their products or services. Craft stores, survival gear, home storage products, cosmetics, home cleaning solutions, etc., have been effectively publicized through free demonstrations or classes. How about your products?

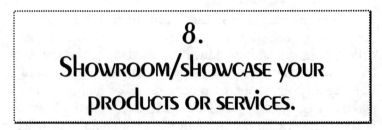

8.
Showroom/showcase your products or services.

Even if your business doesn't sell a tangible product, find something tangible that you can display. Even if you sell only by phone, direct mail or through distributors, have a display of your products neatly arranged in the public part of your office.

Explore the possibility of displaying at the airport or bus station where people often have time to kill. Display cases with tool sets, artwork for sale and executive planners have caught my interest in airports.

Maybe you can get a complementary business to allow you to display your products in their place. For example, a small home furnishings display might work well in a real estate office. Or a showcase for your health spa or sporting goods could be interesting to patrons in a beauty salon.

9.

Train your people well.

Ultimately a company's employees are its best advertisers. Be sure all employees have ample training. The most frequent mistake companies make in seeking short-term savings is to cut training.

Japanese companies often put their people through much more training than we do. I've been told of department store elevator operators who are trained for months so that they know a great deal about people and the store. They can tell you where to find virtually anything in the place. Of course this extensive training makes them much more than simply operators of the lift. They become virtual ambassadors for the store.

Obviously, training need not always be in a classroom setting, although some should be. Assigning more experienced employees to newer ones can create a mentoring relationship as the old hand teaches the rookie what to do. (Be sure the mentor has the best work skills and habits.)

An often overlooked benefit of ongoing training is that it is appreciated by employees. They feel good when their company spends time and money to make them more professional and productive.

10.
Show that you honor customer satisfaction.

A radio station in Florida created a promotion honoring people who give good service. WLKF in Lakeland invites listeners to write to them about great service they witness. Listeners are encouraged to describe the service excellence they see, the name of the company and the name of the person who gave the great service. People cited have their name put into a drawing for a cruise vacation.

I suggested a similar promotion to one of my clients in another part of the country. He contacted a local radio station and arranged to jointly sponsor the contest. The station provided air time while the client's organization funded the prize. The spot on the radio went something like this:

WXXX and Moose Lips Outdoor Stores recognize the importance of good customer service. Better service builds a stronger economic climate throughout Whitebread County. So here's your chance to reward someone who went the extra mile to give you great service.

Send or fax your description of service excellence you've received to WXXX. Be sure to include the name of the business, the date and time of your experience, and the name of the employee who helped you.

Nominated employees will qualify for an all-expense paid cruise on the Mexican Riviera to be given away on March 13.

Join WXXX and Moose Lips Outdoor Stores in celebrating great service!

This joint campaign links your organization with the concept of service excellence. While appearing to be almost a public service, the campaign positions your company as one with a high concern for excellent customer satisfaction.

11.
Use good telephone techniques.

Often your only contact with customers is via the telephone. Make the most of it.

A key to successful phone use is to simply *remember that your customer cannot see you.* Your challenge is to make up for all the lost nonverbal communication by using your voice effectively.

Here are some of the best ways to use the telephone effectively:

♦ **Give the caller your name.** Let the caller know who you are just as you would in a face-to-face situation (via a *name* tag or desk plaque).

♦ **Smile into the phone.** Somehow people can hear a smile over the phone! Some telephone pros place a mirror in front of them while they're on the phone.

♦ **Keep your caller informed.** If you need to look up information, tell the customer what you are doing. Don't leave the caller holding a dead phone with no clue as to whether you are still with him or her.

♦ **Invite the caller to get to the point.** Use questions such as "How can I assist you today?" or "What can I do for you?"

♦ **Commit to requests of the caller.** Tell the caller specifically what you will do and when you will get back to him or her. ("I'll check on this billing problem and get back to you by 5 this afternoon, Okay?")

♦ **Thank the caller.** This lets the caller know when the conversation is over.

♦ **Let your voice fluctuate** in tone, rate and loudness. You hold people's attention by putting a little life into your voice. Express honest reactions in expressive ways. Let your voice tones be natural and friendly.

♦ **Use *hold* carefully.** People hate being put on hold. When it's necessary to use hold, explain why and break in periodically to let your caller know he or she hasn't been forgotten. If what you're doing will take longer than a few minutes, ask the caller if you can call him or her back. *Write down your commitment to call back and don't miss it!*

♦ **Use friendly, tactful words.** Never accuse the customer of anything; never convey that his or her request is an imposition.

For more ideas on phone use, see my book *Winning Telephone Tips*, Career Press, 1997. To order, call the publisher at 800-CAREER-1.

12.
Use word-of-mouth, network sales approaches.

Without reservation, experts agree that word-of-mouth marketing can be the single best way to launch or build a business or professional service. People buy things from people they trust. And trust can be quickly established when someone you regard as credible recommends the business, product or service.

Two major trends will change the face of marketing for the next several years:

1. The intensification of high-tech (online shopping) via the Internet. An increasing number of products are being offered to net users. Purchasing these simply requires a few key strokes and the goods arrive within a few days. This provides tremendous convenience.

2. The second trend is the complement of this impersonal buying behavior: high-touch marketing provided through personalized network marketing. This gives customers a personal relationship with the friends and neighbors who are distributing products.

These two opposite but complementary trends will change the shape of commerce across the world.

Consider these options.

The essence of network marketing is that we provide incentives for other people to sell for us. Full-blown multi-level marketers (MLMs) have elaborate compensation plans that pay several levels of commissions on any sale. You need not go to that extent to gain the advantages of networking. For many businesses, simply rewarding people for referring you is a good start. I've seen many such rewards ranging from giving a customer a free dinner when he or she refers a new customer, to one organization that offers up to a $10,000 finders fee if customers refer new distributors who succeed in the company.

Be creative and think about the multipliers that kick in when you reward others for selling for you.

Don't overlook the power of network marketing. Many experts are predicting that substantial portions of all that we purchase will soon come about by buying from friends and associates.

13.
Ask for referrals.

Always ask a satisfied customer for the names of people who might also like to buy from you. Get addresses and phone numbers and follow through with a call or a card.

While this is a common practice in some industries, it can also be used in hundreds of other situations. Call referred people to introduce yourself and invite them to come to your business. Most people will be surprised and pleased by a personal invitation like that. And it beats sitting around hoping someone will come in.

Of course, the more information you can get about a referred person the better. But don't make referral-giving a big job for your customer. A name and address or phone number is all you need. You can look up other data, if necessary, later.

Bill, my friend in the insurance business, used this line when he has closed a customer: "There are two ways you can pay me in this business. First, I need the names of people you know who could benefit from what I just sold you. Second, I need a check from you." In phrasing it this way, Bill placed heavy importance on the value of the referral. Even before he got the customer's money, he asked for referrals!

Referrals can be that valuable.

14.
...ANd HE Told Two FRIENds, ANd...

Joe Girard claims that everyone knows approximately 250 people. He figures that's about how many people are likely to show up for a typical funeral or wedding. (Joe actually came up with this number by asking funeral directors how many mass cards—with the name and picture of the departed—they typically printed. Funeral directors said "about 250 people" come to pay last respects to the deceased. Weddings are another indicator of the typical person's circle of friends and acquaintances. Again, the number comes out to about 250 for each person. Obviously some people know fewer but many know more, and the number 250 seems a good average figure.)

I don't suggest you start pestering everyone you remotely know to buy your stuff; it probably isn't right for everyone. But starting a prospect list with the names of people you know is always productive.

But, beware! While the 250 acquaintances your customers know may be a great source for you to tap, if you give poor customer service, word will filter out to the 250 people your customer knows and you'll find yourself playing catch-up. Girard illustrates:

> *If I see 50 people in a week, and only two of them are unhappy with the way I treat them, at the end of the year there will be 5,000 people influenced by just those two a week. I've been selling cars for 14 years. So if I turned off just two people a week*

out of all that I see, there would be 70,000 people, a whole stadium full, who know one thing for sure: Don't buy a car from Joe Girard! (Joe Girard, *How to Sell Anything to Anybody*.)

Remember the devastating cost of bad ripple effects. But also remember that the ripples flow both ways. Happy customers will tell their network of friends about your good service, too.

Multilevel or network marketing uses this to maximum advantage by giving customers commissions on sales they have influenced. These compensation plans can get pretty complicated, but here is a simple application anyone can use:

A barber in Detroit has a sign on the wall. It says, "Ask me to explain how you can make $25." When asked, the barber tells his customers that if they refer a friend to a particular car dealership, and the referral eventually buys a car, the dealership will pay them $25. He then gives the customer 10 of the dealership's business cards and puts his or her name and phone number on the back. The barber gets $1 for every card he gives out. This dealership outsold every other dealership in the United States, several years running. (Bill Gallagher, Orvil Ray Wilson, and Jay Conrad Levinson, *Guerrilla Selling,* Houghton Mifflin, 1993, pp. 30-31.)

Does $1 a card seem too high? Maybe not if you are selling $20,000 cars. But the point of the story is that this business was using the principle of networking. Perhaps the barber would do the same task in exchange for free oil changes and minor service on his car.

Make it a practice to look for ways you can network with other people.

....

15.
Give more than just a business card.

Swapping business cards has become a cliché, and, like a cliché, it often goes unnoticed. Here are some ways to boost the effect of giving a card:

1. **Have your card designed** to include your photo. People will remember you.

2. **Print a saying** or quote on the back—something customers will enjoy and remember. (I know one fellow who had a cartoon about his profession on the back of his card.)

3. **Write a personalized note** on it.

4. **Write your home phone number** on it, implying to the receiver an interest in being friends or of your willingness to serve in any way possible.

5. **Staple a brochure** or sample to the card, maybe even a flower.

6. **Clip your card to a newspaper** or magazine article of interest to the recipient.

7. **Display your card prominently** on your desk, counter or with sales literature. Encourage people to take one—or a handful of them—if they might know other interested customers.

8. **Give cards freely.** One company directed that every piece of first-class mail sent out include a business card, even the bills they paid! This led to a call from the local electric company asking about their products. Another fellow literally tossed his cards in the air at football games when the home team scored. Cards do no good sitting in your desk drawer. Get them out.

9. **Offer a bonus** to people who refer your card to friends. Have them write their name on the back and when a prospect comes in showing the card, reward the person who gave it to the prospect.

Let creativity be your guide. I read about a woman who wanted to expand her accounting practice, so she bought a small ad in her local newspaper. She had the printer leave the ad blank except for a line across the bottom asking readers to file her business card for future reference. As the papers came off the press, she and her husband stuck her photo business card into the blank space with double-stick tape. Months later she was still hearing from readers. Do not try this with *The New York Times,* of course. (This and lots of other good ideas are found in *Guerrilla Selling.*)

16.
Take advantage of new technology.

Businesses of all sizes and types now have a wider array of technology available than ever before. Try some of these:

1. **Fax on demand.** Install phone lines that allow your customers to contact you through their fax machines to receive your messages "on demand." Here you can provide updated information, new product offerings, details on product or service changes, etc. And you can get your customers a detailed description with no labor costs.

2. **Use 800, 888, 900 numbers and pagers.** Make it easy for people to contact you. Today's telephone services can easily provide you with numbers that are toll free to the caller (800 and 888 numbers) or 900 numbers that bill the customer for calling. These 900 numbers can be established with recorded messages or live operators, although the latter is obviously more expensive. Such numbers may bill callers up to $4 or $5 per minute for specialized information and become a profit center in themselves. The allure of 900 numbers, however, is diminishing as more people use Internet web pages. Pagers can also provide a customer with instant access, thus making them feel more closely connected to you—if you answer the pages received promptly.

3. **Web pages.** Create a web page on the Internet that provides customers with information about your organization. Make the page attractive and professional looking. Be sure to employ a web master (someone to regularly update the page with the latest information) and then send out e-mail inviting people to visit your page.

4. **Try targeted bulk e-mail.** Internet users quickly become upset with junk e-mail sent to virtually everyone of a service provider's membership. The response rates are tiny, but the cost of sending a message to literally millions of people can make up for the poor response. A better approach is to purchase targeted lists of net users who may be interested in what you are selling. E-mail list providers (just as regular mailing list providers) can help you target specific groups or specific demographic characteristics, thus greatly improving your likely response rate.

17.
Build and maintain a prospect list.

Prospecting isn't just for insurance salespeople. Try it.

Make a list including everyone you can think of who might need your products or services. Don't be too selective. Think about every situation where you come across different people. List friends, business associates, members of organizations you belong to, old school friends, people you buy products and services from, and more.

Whether you use a computer or a large legal pad, put one name on each line. If you have phone numbers and addresses, fine. But get the name down even if you'll need to look up additional information in order to contact the person.

Look at your list regularly, anytime you have a break in business from the customers you are serving. Add to the list often as new people come to mind.

Once people on the list become real prospects (they have a need or have indicated some interest) "promote" them to your card file or to a prospect file on your computer. Then use *this file* for follow-up. A number of contact manager software packages are available through which you can capture all kinds of personalized data and recent conversation notes.

Don't just wait for people to wander into your place of business. Contact *them*. Make it a habit to reach out to potential customers every day.

I knew a young man I'll call Tom, who came out of the military service and decided that he wanted to run his own business. He had no experience and wasn't even sure what he'd do. He just knew that he wanted to be his own boss.

For his first venture, Tom worked a deal with a wholesaler of small appliances. Tom could get good-quality products at very attractive prices. He set up a small store and, at first, did what almost every other store owner does: He ran a few newspaper ads and waited for customers to come in and buy.

Guess what? They didn't.

Tom was an impatient sort. A take-charge guy. So, instead of sitting around waiting, he created a list of people he knew and began calling them. His pitch to them was low-key. He simply told the truth: He had started a new business and it was going pretty slow. He wondered if they knew of anyone who might have a need for a small appliance.

In other words, he just asked for the business.

Wow! What a revolutionary idea! Of course it isn't. It's common sense, yet how many small store owners do you know who do this?

Tom's story has a happy ending as you might guess. He succeeded in his first store and went on to develop a chain of appliance stores that have earned him a handsome living.

18.
BE A good CITIZEN.

Be a corporate good citizen and your efforts will be rewarded. Indirect advertising via sponsorship of community events is a good way to plant the name of your company in the minds of potential customers.

Jack, a good friend of mine, has a clear set of corporate values. He is dedicated to producing and distributing high-quality products at modest costs, while giving a portion of his profits back to his community.

Jack has chosen a local charity that he feels strongly about—the Easter Seals Foundation—and he looks for opportunities to help them. At Christmas time he sends his customers, suppliers and other business associates a letter wishing them a happy holiday season and indicating that he has made a contribution to the Easter Seals Foundation in their name. A few days later, these same people get a letter from the charity acknowledging the gift Jack made in their name. A double reminder of Jack's goodwill!

Recently Jack helped organize a golf tournament to benefit his favorite charity. His suppliers were invited to "sponsor a hole" for a donation of $500. At the designated hole appeared a small sign acknowledging the supplier's donation.

This low key, responsive advertising can be more powerful than loud TV spots.

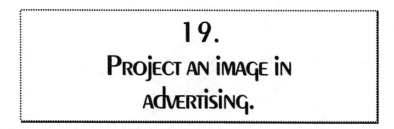

19.
PROJECT AN IMAGE IN ADVERTISING.

Advertising materials get much more bang for the buck if they look somewhat alike. Use the same company logo, slogans, colors and themes. Changing these too often confuses the customer.

Keep your advertising theme simple. Select slogans or mottoes that clearly and simply state what your company stands for. The fewer words, the better.

Look at the advertising giants. Coca-Cola, Pepsi, Procter & Gamble, auto manufacturers, TV networks, etc. They always have simple, short ad slogans. Likewise, the giant retailers who use "Satisfaction guaranteed" or "Where America Shops" to convey a simple message. One of my favorites is from Land's End, the direct merchant clothing giant. It's motto is, "Guaranteed. Period." That's it. Two words that say a mouthful.

If you don't have an ad slogan or organizational theme, get your people together and come up with one. (See Paul R. Timm, *50 Powerful Ideas You Can Use to Keep Your Customers,* Career Press, 1992, pp. 46-50.)

If you use radio or TV spots, get credible, professional voices to speak your message. About 25 percent of people have an "auditory predisposition," meaning they prefer to receive sensory input via listening. Be sure your spokesperson's voice doesn't turn them off.

20.
BROADCAST YOUR SUCCESSES.

Let people know how you help customers. Let people know about situations when you have helped customers identify applications for your products that may be unusual.

Use the business press. Columnists for local newspapers are constantly looking for new material. If you have an interesting story to tell, contact them. A phone call will usually tell you whether you have something they'd be interested in.

Journalists need stories, and if you have a story or a new product, service or application, they will be interested.

If you are uncomfortable with a cold phone call, write a press release and then follow up with a call.

If you aren't good at writing or don't have the time, contact a nearby university's journalism or communication department. Ask if there are students who would like some "real-world" experience in writing press releases. Many students will jump at the opportunity. Pay them a few dollars for any releases that make the news.

Broadcasting doesn't have to involve the mass media. Post a bulletin board with photos of new customers (pictured with your product) and letters that compliment your company. If a particularly good letter comes in, call the writer and ask if it could be used in your advertising. Then run an ad showing the letter.

21.
List your business in phone directories.

Yellow pages are a must for any business that deals with the general public. You need not have the largest ad, but you do need to be listed. You should also take advantage of listing opportunities in professional directories or memberships.

Better still, use the directories available to locate customers. A trip to your local business library will be time well spent. Learn what kinds of directories are available. If you sell to other businesses, books like the Dun & Bradstreet *Million Dollar Directory* or *MacRae's Blue Book* will give you basic information about every business in a particular region. Generally you can get the names of key people (including purchasing agents), branch and home office locations, and even their credit ratings. You can then contact the companies about your products, or better yet, gather information about them that may give you tips on how to meet their needs.

Another directory used by savvy business people is *R. L. Polk City Directory* found at the library's reference desk. This book lists every household (denoting home owners) and business by address and lots of additional information. New home owners and businesses are also noted.

Finally, while you are at the library, review trade journals that target your industry. Look for feature articles that show what successful people are doing.

Read with the intent of gathering new ideas or applications you can use.

22.
Check out trade shows, fairs and flea markets.

As with anything, there are tricks to this trade show business. A lot of people think they can just set up a table with a display and customers will flock to them. Sorry, it's not that simple.

Here are some tips from the pros:

1. **Pre-invite potential customers to visit your booth.** Get lists of convention attendees in advance, if possible. Send them a letter of invitation and a card they can redeem at your booth for a prize or gift. When I was president of a training company, we told convention attendees that if they brought the letter we sent them to our booth and viewed our seven-minute introductory video, they'd receive a free calculator. When the expo opened, people came running!

2. **Make your giveaway prominent.** Example: A computer software producer selling a tape backup system (so you wouldn't lose stored data) gave away a kid's bank shaped like a safe. This six-inch cube was pretty bulky to carry around the expo, but people who saw others with it asked how they could get one too. The prize attracted attention and tied in with the company's product theme.

3. **Work the booth!** Instruct all employees working at the booth that this is not a passive venture. Don't sit down. Greet all guests. Pre-plan an opening gambit to create interest.

4. **Follow up all leads.** Quickly contact any leads you get from the booth. The key word here is *quickly*. Prospect leads get cold very fast.

23.
CROSS-PROMOTE WITH ANOTHER business.

Tire dealer Les Schwab built his highly successful business in the Pacific Northwest. In the early 1960s, Les hatched an idea with the Oregon Cattlemen's Association to give beef certificates to tire buyers. In his autobiography, he describes his "free beef" promotion:

> *It has been one of our most successful promotions in that it helps to promote the sale of beef, and also the sale of tires. From almost the first day of my business I had made up my mind that I wanted the business of the rancher. I can safely say that ranchers have been the backbone of my business for 34 years. I have specialized in ranch tires from car tires, pickup tires, truck, tractor and oddball sizes to fit various ranch equipment.* (Les Schwab, *Les Schwab Pride in Performance,* Bend, Oregon: Maverick Publishers, 1986, p. 47.)

Tire buyers received a $7.50 to $15 certificate toward the purchase of beef, depending on how many tires they bought. Most customers bought even more beef than the free certificate allowed. Schwab cross-promoted by:

1. Identifying a key group of customers (ranchers).

2. Finding a way to promote their interests.

3. Creating a feeling of partnership.

24.
Publish a book.

A friend of mine published a paperback book called *How to Avoid Auto Service Ripoffs*. Guess what business he is in? His book bore a $7.95 price tag but was either sold at a deep discount in his shop or given away. The book had many tips, but its more important function was that it told customers that they wouldn't be ripped off at his business.

People trust what they see in print. A publication projects credibility and trust.

Isn't writing a book a lot of work? Sure. But there are people who can help you. Check with a university's journalism or public relations program to see if there are students with good writing skills who would like a chance to become a published author. After you've seen samples of the students' writing, negotiate a flat fee (typically a few hundred dollars will do it) and tell the writer that he or she will be listed as a coauthor.

Then sit down with your tape recorder and spill your guts. Give the tapes to the hired writer and watch his or her youthful enthusiasm have at it.

Use this space to generate your own ideas on how to **attract** *new customers.*

_____

_____

_____

_____

_____

_____

_____

_____

_____

_____

_____

_____

_____

_____

50 Powerful Ways to Win New Customers

*Use this space to generate your own ideas on how to **attract** new customers.*

_____

_____

_____

_____

_____

_____

_____

_____

_____

_____

_____

_____

_____

*Use this space to generate your own ideas on how to **attract** new customers.*

_____

_____

_____

_____

_____

_____

_____

_____

_____

_____

_____

_____

_____

_____

50 Powerful Ways to Win New Customers

Use this space to generate your own ideas on how to **attract** *new customers.*

_____

_____

_____

_____

_____

_____

_____

_____

_____

_____

_____

_____

_____

_____

Part 2

Motivate Customers

Two classes of action will motivate potential customers to try the products or services of your business or organization:

1. Offering specific incentives.

2. Inciting customers to immediate action.

25.
Use coupon books or punch cards for repeat customers.

A few months ago, a woman came to my door selling a coupon booklet for a local dry cleaner. The booklet offered some $200 worth of discounts and cost $35. She offered to sell it to me for just $29. I checked her references (which she cheerfully provided) and realized that the dry cleaner was one I occasionally used. So I bought it.

Then I asked how this promotion worked. She explained that she got to keep a substantial part of the $29 and that the cleaner absorbed the remaining discounts by increasing customer traffic—a win-win situation.

An auto repair shop used a similar approach with a twist. It printed up coupon books and donated them to the local high school. High school kids then sold the booklets and kept the proceeds. The repair business built traffic and increased its customer base. Its costs in the short term were more than made up for in repeat customers.

Be sure your business is ready to handle increased customer loads and, by all means, be sure all employees are informed about the promotion. Nothing kills the benefits of such an effort faster than having a clerk who responds, "I can't accept those coupons."

26.
DONATE TO A CHARITY
WHEN NEW CUSTOMERS TRY YOU.

Researchers have found that they can significantly increase the likelihood of response to a survey when they offer a donation to charity for each returned survey. Even compared against surveyors who enclose 50 cents or a dollar as a token of appreciation, the charity approach works better. The cash reward is too small to be meaningful to recipients but they feel good about the charitable donation.

A similar approach can be used to get new customers to look at your company. Offer a donation for a test drive or demonstration of your product. Better yet, give your customers a choice of three different charities.

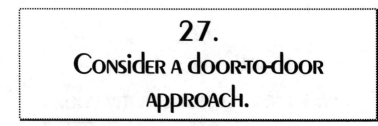

27.
Consider a door-to-door approach.

Door-to-door sales can work well, especially if your customers don't expect to be reached in this way.

Try canvassing homes or businesses nearby. Use an informational, friendly approach, not a hard sell. Simply let people know that you are in the neighborhood and would appreciate their business.

If people are not home or prefer not to talk, just leave a flyer or brochure.

So few people do door-to-door business anymore that it creates an element of surprise. Be sure to be sensitive to privacy, and avoid canvassing at times when people might consider your appearance an interruption. Keep it low-key and nonthreatening.

28.
TRY A LETTER CAMPAIGN.

A variation of phone or door-to-door prospecting is a letter campaign. For almost every business, there are people out there who would be happy to buy from you *if they only knew you were available to them.*

I often think about the process of buying an automobile. For most of us it's a rather unpleasant task. Cars cost a lot of money and we want to feel certain that we are getting a good value. We feel best about this when we are buying from someone we trust and like—when we buy from a friend.

Don't you wish you had a trusted friend in the car business? For most of us, we never will have such a friend unless we go to the dealership and make a friend. Initiating such a friendship is uncomfortable for most people.

The alert car salesperson sees the opportunity to get new customers by building friendships. Such people are active in community, church, civic or volunteer groups and aren't bashful about letting people know that they sell cars.

You don't have to be an aggressive, high-pressure salesperson to make such contacts in your community. In fact, your approach should be exactly the opposite. Make friends first, then make it easy for your friends to do business with you.

A friendly letter like this one may work wonders:

(Date)

Dear Betty:

Just a note to tell you how much I enjoy working with you in the Soup Kitchen (or Rotary Club, or Church Youth Program or whatever). I value your friendship and feel good about what we have been able to accomplish together.

If I can ever be of help to you in purchasing a car (or insurance or computer or business services or whatever you sell), please give me a call.

Again, thanks for your friendship. See you next Tuesday.

Regards,

Tom

Tom

Would people be insulted or offended by such a note? Very rarely. It's low-key and expresses appreciation for the reader while simply reminding individuals that you would welcome them as customers. Enclose a couple of business cards with the letter.

And remember the undertaker's motto: "Everybody will be a customer someday. Make friends and they'll be your customer."

Use this space to generate your own ideas on how to
motivate *your customers.*

_____

_____

_____

_____

_____

_____

_____

_____

_____

_____

_____

_____

50 Powerful Ways to Win New Customers

Use this space to generate your own ideas on how to ***motivate*** *your customers.*

_____

_____

_____

_____

_____

_____

_____

_____

_____

_____

_____

_____

_____

_____

Use this space to generate your own ideas on how to **motivate** *your customers.*

_____

_____

_____

_____

_____

_____

_____

_____

_____

_____

_____

_____

_____

_____

50 Powerful Ways to Win New Customers

*Use this space to generate your own ideas on how to **motivate** your customers.*

_____

_____

_____

_____

_____

_____

_____

_____

_____

_____

_____

_____

Part 3

Retain Current Customers

Two kinds of actions will greatly increase your chances for building customer loyalty and repeat business:

1. Exceed customer expectations.

2. Improve your customer service constantly.

29.
Apply E-Plus: The master key to customer satisfaction.

There is no more powerful way to win repeat customers than to *exceed* their expectations. E-Plus is the term I use to remind people of this process:

1. Constantly strive to sharpen your understanding of what customers want from you. Be specific and objective.

2. Consistently seek ideas for exceeding these expectations.

Let me put on my psychologist's hat for a moment here and explain why E-Plus is so powerful.

Customers are rational people. If a buying experience is positive, they might come back; if negative, they'll try to avoid returning. The challenge is to improve the probability that they will come back. But customers who are satisfied may be inert, not motivated. Their satisfaction simply means the *absence of dissatisfaction,* not the motivation to become a repeat customer. The challenge, then, is to get beyond satisfaction to motivation.

The crucial role of customer expectations

Customers entering into a transaction, bring a range of expectations (albeit perhaps unconsciously) about what the transaction will be like. What they expect is based on past experience with your business or ones like it. These mental expectations are *perceptual*. They exist in the mind of the customer. Sometimes they are accurate and rational; sometimes they aren't.

Perceptions of customer satisfaction go beyond just the quality of the core product or service. They take into account the whole buying experience. Expectations will vary among different organizations or under differing circumstances. For example, people expect different treatment from a full-service retailer than they do from a warehouse store. They won't expect the same service from a prestigious law firm and a state auto license bureau.

Different expectations from different businesses

Suppose you intend to shop at a low-cost, self-service, discount store. Going into the store, you anticipate a certain kind of experience. You do not necessarily expect that the clerk (if you can find one) in the clothing department will be an expert in fitting clothing. Nor would you expect that person to be particularly helpful in coordinating items you may want to purchase. This is not to say that some people who work there would not have these skills, but you probably wouldn't expect this as a general rule.

If you simply select some clothing items from a rack and take them to a checkout for purchase, you are not surprised, nor particularly disappointed. That is about what you expected, and if other aspects of the store are satisfactory (it seems clean and well-stocked, for instance) you could be perfectly satisfied.

By contrast, if you go to a high-quality, high-service clothing store or a boutique, you expect a different kind of transaction. You probably expect to be served by people who have expertise in clothing fit, color and materials. You might realistically expect personal attention and assistance as you make your purchases.

One of three situations—negative, neutral or positive—will result as customers compare their expectations with the service received:

Negative	**Neutral**	**Positive**
• Positive expectations failed.	• Expectations met.	• Negative expectations failed.
• Negative expectations confirmed.		• Positive or neutral expectations exceeded.

In the situation described in the left column, the customer's experience was worse than expected. She's dissatisfied and likely to defect to another provider, if she has a rational alternative. The middle-column customer is neither dissatisfied nor particularly motivated to return.

In the right-column situation, the transaction was better than expected. Either the customer thought it would be pretty good—and it was *very* good, or the customer thought it would not be very good but it was better than expected. If positive expectations were sufficiently exceeded (or negative ones shown to be unfounded), this customer is a good candidate for repeat business. The right-column situation is an E-Plus experience—customer expectations were *exceeded*.

Why E-Plus leads to customer retention

A social psychological theory called Equity Theory explains why we can predict that the E-Plus (right-column) customer will become a repeat customer.

Equity Theory considers all kinds of social relationships ranging from the intimate to the cursory. The buyer-seller situation is one such relationship.

In any relationship, people constantly assess the fairness or relative *equity* of their involvement compared to other relationships. Psychologically, people regularly check to see if what they give to the relationship balances with what they get out of it.

The theory predicts what people will do when they perceive inequity. When the person thinks the business is getting the better deal in this relationship, the customer will respond with one or some combination of the following:

♦ Ignore or rationalize the inequity. The customer concludes that the service is poor but it's poor everywhere. The world isn't fair but it's not worth fighting it.

♦ Demand restitution. The offended person demands fairer treatment, or the customer wants his money back.

♦ Retaliation. The offended person speaks badly of the organization or person seen as the cause of the inequity. Outright sabotage is an extreme form of retaliation.

♦ Withdraw from the relationship. The customer refuses to do further business with the organization or person.

Hence, the dissatisfied customer is likely to do one of these things. The first two alternatives may give a business a chance to patch things up and retain the customer. But the last two can be devastating.

Customers often retaliate for perceived inequity by telling other people about poor service received. The typical unhappy customer tells 10 to 20 others about his or her experience, studies say. These negative ripple effects can result in scores or even hundreds of lost customers or potential customers.

But there is another side to Equity Theory that predicts this: People who feel that they are receiving more than they *deserve* from a transaction also experience a psychological need to restore balance. A simple example is the social pressure you might feel to reciprocate after being invited to someone's home for dinner. The relationship will remain unbalanced until you equalize it with a similar kindness.

Herein lies the theoretical basis for exceeding customer expectations. By going beyond the expected, you create an imbalance that, for many people, requires action on their part to rebalance. They may rationalize or ignore it, of course. But attempts to restore the balance can also take the form of:

♦ Telling others of the positive experience.

♦ Paying a premium for the goods received.

♦ Becoming a repeat customer.

The challenge, then, is to create positive imbalances by exceeding customer expectations. This is E-Plus.

Explain E-Plus to all employees. Then schedule regular brainstorming sessions where everyone can have fun coming up with new E-Plus ideas.

The next several ideas show specific areas where you can create E-Plus experiences.

30.
E-Plus with added value.

When I ask people to describe value that exceeds their expectations, I hear tales of exceptional products like 15-year-old Kirby vacuum cleaners and 20-year-old Western Auto freezers. Often people talk about their Ford or Toyota pickup truck with 200,000 miles on it, or a sweater that dates back a quarter century. These products exceeded the customers' expectations of value. They got more than they expected for their money.

Value is determined by the quality of the product relative to its price. If the product is inexpensive, say a 79-cent ball point pen, you may not be too upset if it quits working in a few weeks. But if you buy a $79 pen, you expect it to last for years. Herein lies a problem in creating E-Plus in the area of value: Something of value does not become evident until long after the product is bought.

Some actions, however, can convey quality immediately. Something as simple as packaging can enhance the perceived value. Stores that gift-wrap goods or provide customers with high-quality shopping bags can project additional value.

A department store where I shop always gives me a vinyl, zip-up hanger bag when I buy a suit or sportcoat. Some bookstores and gift shops have attractive and sophisticated wrapping paper for goods sold. These can create E-Plus in customer's minds.

Keep in mind that E-Plus has two sides to it: the expected and the received. Be sure your customers have realistic expectations about your products. If they unrealistically expect something to last 10 years and it's only designed to last five, be sure to clarify that.

How can *your* business give more value than expected?

31.
E-Plus with added information.

My son recently had knee surgery. The therapist not only explained what exercises he should do but also gave him photocopied sheets illustrating exactly how do them. She wrote his name at the top of each sheet and numbered the sequence.

Enlightened auto salespeople spend time with the customer, after the sale, explaining all the features on the new car. The last vehicle I bought came with a cassette tape that explained all the truck's features and maintenance tips. A hospital client changed the signs and installed color stripes on the corridor floors to direct people to various departments. A cellular phone dealer calls customers to see if they understand how to use their phone's features and offers to meet to explain them in person.

E-Plus often means providing information in a more usable or personalized form. Companies might provide instructional videos, hands-on lessons, or step-by-step checklists. Many have gone to 800/888 numbers for customer assistance or advice. Some provide users with newsletters or new application ideas for their product.

How can *your* business give customers more useful information?

32.
E-Plus with better speed.

A well-known air freight company claims to deliver packages by 10 a.m. the next morning, but they often arrive by 9 a.m. or 9:30 a.m. The repair office for a major office equipment company makes it a point to have the service person arrive earlier than promised.

At a supermarket, additional cashiers open when more than two customers are in line. Some fast-food restaurants have your lunch up almost before you can order it.

Incidentally, my research into customer "pet peeves" has shown clearly that the number one turnoff is slow or inefficient service. Even restaurants where you might expect leisurely dining to be the expectation were downgraded in the mind of customers if the service was perceived as too slow. (For a condensed report of research findings, see Paul R. Timm and Kristen DeTienne's "From Slogans to Strategy: A Workable Approach to Customer Satisfaction and Loyalty," in *EXCHANGE*, a publication of the Marriott School of Management, Brigham Young University, Spring 1993.)

Are there ways *you* can give the customer faster service than he or she expects?

33.
E-Plus with personality.

Every organization projects a "personality" to its customers. If people find the personality pleasing and helpful, they come back. If the personality seems aloof, uncaring, or even hostile (as some companies do), the customer will do all possible to avoid returning.

This personality is projected mostly via nonverbal and verbal communication behaviors of the employees. Below are some ideas for projecting a favorable personality:

1. **Greet customers immediately** and by name if possible. People coming to your place of business are on strange turf; they are likely to feel somewhat uncomfortable until you greet them. You wouldn't have a guest come to your home only to be ignored, yet some businesses do exactly that to their customers. Even if your employees are working with another customer, make eye contact and say hello to the customer who comes in.

2. **Be aware of the impact of body positioning** and touch. Standing or sitting too close to customers can make them uncomfortable. Positioning yourself too far away can make you seem aloof and uninterested. Shaking hands or other appropriate touching can strengthen a relationship. (Be careful, of course, to keep within culturally accepted standards.)

3. **Don't allow a telephone interruption** to distract you from the customer in front of you. Ask the caller to hold or offer to call him back rather than ignore the customer you are waiting on.

4. **Say "please" and "thank you."** This sounds a bit like one of those kindergarten books, but the principle holds. Be polite and respectful. Make "thank you" the last words the customer hears from you. Even if they don't buy, thank them for visiting or considering your company. (Incidentally, be careful to avoid substitutes for these words. Saying "there you go" to a customer upon completion of a transaction is not the same as saying "thank you."

5. **Use lively voice tones** on the phone. Hire telephone people who can project a positive personality over the telephone. Use variation in pitch, rate and loudness to convey feeling.

6. **Avoid jargon** or specialized terms your customer may not understand. When people hear an unfamiliar term, they have two choices: to ask for clarification or fake understanding. Most people opt for the second one. Check your customer's understanding periodically and look for nonverbal cues that you may not be communicating very clearly. If your customer looks confused, ask if they understand or rephrase your information in another way.

7. **Respect people's time.** Be prompt and efficient in dealing with customers. The number one pet peeve I hear expressed by customers is slow or inefficient service. Being respectful of time conveys a very positive personality quality.

8. Use customers' names. Few things sound better to a customer than to have someone call him or her by name—respectfully. When in doubt about whether to use a person's first name or remain more formal using the last name, opt for on the side formality. They can always invite you to use their first name later. You can get people's names off their checks, credit cards, or your appointment schedule.

An organization's personality arises from these and myriad other factors. If your company is a friendly, enjoyable place to work and employs friendly, upbeat people, your customers' expectations will be exceeded.

34.
E-Plus with add-ons.

A shoe store clerk gives a shoehorn and asks if the customer would like to try padded inserts or lifetime guarantee socks. (Sometimes add-ons are sold, sometimes given away.) A clerk at a supermarket hands customers a few candy kisses with the receipt—an unexpected thank you. The paint store clerk checks to be sure the customer has caulking and sandpaper, which might have been forgotten.

One of my favorites: The drive-in teller at a bank has long given lollipops to kids in the car, but now offers a dog biscuit to customers with dogs in the car.

My son refuses to rent videos anywhere except the place that gave *him* a free bag of popcorn. I always fill the car's tank where I get a free car wash. The costs of these add-ons? I'm told the popcorn costs 4 cents and the car wash 7 cents. Those pennies buy a lot of customer loyalty.

Advertising specialties or free gifts have been shown to be "bang-up marketing tools for all demographic groups," according to Jay Conrad Levinson (Jay Conrad Levinson, "Free for All," *Entrepreneur*, May 1997, p.94.) Giveaways that carry your company's logo or a message do seem to have an impact so long as the gift is regarded as useful or interesting. Studies show that 40 percent of people remember the name of the advertiser as long as six months after receiving a free gift. And 31 percent still use the gift one year after receiving it.

35.
E-Plus with convenience.

The fastest growing businesses are those that offer added convenience. It wasn't too many years ago when getting the oil changed in your car meant leaving the vehicle all day at a service station. Today, lube centers will do the job in 15 minutes while you wait in a comfortable area.

Pizza would not likely be America's favorite food if it were not for quick home or office delivery. I visited a tie store that offered to deliver a tie to my office (in case I got razzed about the ugly one I wore or had an important meeting come up). This same store has a "tie of the month" promotion. They send customers a color photocopied sheet showing several of the newest offerings. The customer calls, and the tie is delivered.

Convenience is especially important when dealing with a product problem. The typical response to a customer with a faulty product is "bring it in and we'll replace it." That is E but not E-Plus.

Toyota's Lexus division did it better when handling a recall. Dealerships called customers for an appointment to pick up the car. They left a loaner car, and some dealerships even left a rose or a $50 bill on the seat to apologize for the inconvenience! The outcome? Customers were exposed to the exceptional service department, and an embarrassment became what one Toyota executive called "a watershed event" for getting customers into the dealership's shop.

Some young friends of mine took the quick lube oil change service a step further and developed "Valet Oil Service." With specially equipped vans they now go to customers' homes or work locations and change oil and make minor auto repairs. Their computer keeps track of the customers' cars and mileage so that they'll know when to change the oil again. All this happens without any inconvenience to the car owners.

E-Plussing in the area of convenience can be a particularly fruitful strategy in today's busy world.

You can contact the Speciality Advertising Association International for access to more than 4,000 members. Or you may want to check the yellow pages for specialty advertisers to get on some mailing lists. Select creative and interesting items if you decide to use this approach.

One of the simplest E-Plus ideas I've seen is done regularly by my favorite lunch restaurant. Periodically, they simply give lunch for free to regular customers. Each of their counter employees are empowered to give away a number of free lunches. When they do, the customer is delighted and surprised—and well on the way to becoming a loyal customer.

36.
Identify and improve your POEs.

Make a list of each of your company's *points of encounter* (POEs) with customers or potential customers. Then focus your efforts on making these POEs smooth, professional and pleasant.

Your customer's POEs probably include the point at which he:

1. First hears about your business or becomes aware of what you do.

2. Makes contact with you either in person or by phone.

3. Waits to be served.

4. Is introduced to your products or services.

5. Tries out your product.

6. Experiences your follow-up.

7. Encounters the way you handle problems.

What potential problems might the customer face at each of these POEs?

For the first POE, he may not be clear as to what you do, or may have concerns about your ability or willingness to help him. He may be impressed (favorably or negatively) with your organization's logo, slogans, work location or the like.

For the second POE, the customer may be put off by appearances or mannerisms that project low professionalism or unfriendliness.

For the third POE, he may be frustrated by delays or the boredom of having to wait. (Walt Disney World spent a lot of effort developing ways to reduce the boredom of waiting in lines for rides. My local post office installed displays of interesting stamps and even a videotape player to keep its customers distracted.) Restaurants provide music or light reading. The Marriott hotel even posts the day's newspaper above the urinals in the men's room to keep us busy folks occupied!

The fourth and fifth POEs involve the people skills of your customer contact people. Getting people to try the product immediately has a very positive impact on selling and satisfying. Computer dealers who sit the prospect down and have *him* punch a few keys and car dealers who get him in for a test drive are making the most of these POEs.

The sixth and seventh POEs can do a great deal to create a loyal repeat customer.

Think about your customer's POEs. (There may be others in addition to these seven.) Then make these as smooth and professional as possible.

37.
Make your office customer-friendly.

Be sensitive to layout and decor. Check for barriers. Often people arrange their workspace so that there is a desk or table between them and the customer. While sometimes this is necessary, often it creates an unnecessary barrier. Try inviting customers to sit beside your desk with you instead of across from you. Try using a small round table, especially when customers need to read materials you give them.

Some auto dealerships removed all sales office desks and replaced them with small round tables. Now the customer and salesperson sit around the table and work *together* to make a deal.

Finally, look for customer comfort. Are your customers invited to sit in a comfortable chair? Does your office or store invite them to relax? Are waiting areas furnished with reading materials, soothing music, perhaps a TV? Are vending machines available? Is the vending area kept clean?

A small auto body shop I visited surprised me. It had a waiting room that looked like a living room. Easy chairs, a TV, coffee table with magazines, even fresh flowers. Take a look at your work areas from the customer's viewpoint.

Incidentally, I heard of an interesting layout idea used by the manager who handled the more serious complaints at a business. He mounted a large mirror behind his desk so that irate complainers had to see themselves as he saw them. This cooled off a lot of people!

38.
GET TO KNOW YOUR
"A" CUSTOMERS.

The ever-popular 80/20 Rule—80 percent of your business will come from 20 percent of your customers—really does have validity. (Also, 80 percent of your profits will come from 20 percent of your products, but that's another story.) Get to know those crucial 20 percenters, your "A" customers, that account for most of your success.

Ironically, some businesses don't have much respect for their "A" customers. Banking executives, for example, sometimes look upon people with high debt with some disdain, yet people who owe banks money are their best customers. Candy shop or toy store owners who get irritated with kids may be griping about their best customers. And retailers who prejudge a customer's ability to buy are often dumbfounded when someone not matching their "profile" turns out to be a legitimate "A" customer.

I recently talked with a man who had a $4 million line of credit at a local bank. This fellow was not known for sartorial splendor (he dressed like a slob). When he asked a teller for some crisp $10 bills to give his grandchildren, she gave *him* a hard time. He was patient, but when she refused to stamp his parking ticket, he went to a nearby officer and inquired about the possibility of withdrawing his funds.

When the officer saw who it was, some serious tap dancing took place and the account was saved. But the teller wasn't. She became a casualty of ignorance and poor service compounded by being unaware of an "A" customer.

39.
ANTICIPATE CUSTOMER NEEDS.

Helen, a middle-aged woman, was hired to work in a local department store during the Christmas season. During a particularly hectic day, a young, pregnant mother with two toddlers holding onto her approached Helen's cash register. Spotting the woman, Helen excused herself from the other customers for a moment and took a chair from behind the counter to the young woman.

"Why don't you sit down here," she asked, "and I'll ring up your purchases in a few minutes and bring them back to you."

The shopper was astounded and appreciative!

All Helen had done was *anticipate customer needs* and then did something about them. She won a loyal customer for that store through her initiative and good sense.

Other ways we might anticipate and meet needs:

♦ **Be sure the customer has everything needed** to use the product. (If he buys paint, for example, ask if he has enough brushes, thinner, sandpaper, etc.)

♦ **Offer to carry merchandise** to the customer's car.

♦ **Help reduce confusion.** If an application form is difficult, show your customer which parts he needs to complete and you fill in the rest.

♦ **Respond to the customer's urgency.** If she's in a hurry, work quickly to accommodate.

♦ **Be sure your customer has enough information** to use the product or service. (If written directions or clarification would be useful, write some and provide photocopies to customers.)

♦ **Make your work place barrier-free** and easily accessible. Open areas look better and allow easier communication.

♦ **Be available** when your customers need you. Years ago, banks closed at 2 p.m. and most stores by 6 p.m. People today expect more. Car dealerships are starting to have extended service department hours (some even 24 hours!) Government agencies have been notorious for being open when working people can't get there, but that, too, is improving.

♦ **Have large, clear signs** both inside and outside your business place.

40.
Help your customers feel at home.

A small college bookstore in rural Ohio was featured in a story in *The Wall Street Journal* because it offered a special homey feeling. It offered something the large discount chains cannot: a second living room.

The story reports that "here customers can sit in armchairs, eat Ben & Jerry's ice cream and read all day without buying a thing. They can even leaf through magazines, make a copy of an article and put the publication back on the shelf—without getting a cold stare from an employee" ("College Bookstore Invites Its Customers to Curl Up," *The Wall Street Journal,* Aug. 27, 1992, p. B2.).

Does this make good business sense? The store manager thinks so. He believes that customers buy more when there is no pressure to buy. "The more we seem to try *not* to sell things, the more we sell," he says. He attributes the low-pressure approach to helping him quadruple sales over the past 10 years.

The store also became a place where students and faculty members could relax and chat over a cup of coffee. In short, this store tries to make people feel at home.

41.
CONSIDER THE POSSIBILITY OF DOING AWAY WITH SALESPEOPLE.

Buying an automobile has long been a stressful experience for people. It's a large-ticket item and customers often feel they are getting skinned, especially if they are not skilled negotiators.

Saturn Division of General Motors was one of the first to go to fixed pricing on cars. The sticker price is actually what the car costs. (A revolutionary idea!?) But because the price is not negotiated, customers deal with product information specialists, not salespeople. The customer knows what the car will cost; the employee teaches about the features and benefits of the product.

Ford has applied a similar policy to the sale of its Escort cars and many individual dealerships are going to fixed pricing. In many cases, salespeople are taken off commission and paid a fixed salary. The company's culture changes and customers feel more comfortable.

The same principle can apply to any business where people have traditionally felt some sales pressure. Another step may be to put salespeople on salary rather than commission and give bonuses for exceptional customer support.

42.
Listen with more than your ears.

There is no such thing as an unpopular listener. Almost everyone becomes more interesting when he stops talking. Pay attention to your talk-listen ratio. Are you giving the customer equal time or better?

To be a better listener, use these ideas:

- ♦ **Judge the content** of what people are saying, *not the way they are saying it.* Customers may not have the "right" words, but they know what they need better than anyone.

- ♦ **Hold your fire.** Don't jump to make judgments before your customer has finished talking.

- ♦ **Work at listening.** Maintain eye contact and discipline yourself to listen to what is being said. Tune out those thoughts that get you thinking about something else.

- ♦ **Resist distractions.** Make the customer the center of your attention.

- ♦ **Seek clarification** from customers so you fully understand their needs. Do this in a nonthreatening way using sincere, open-ended questions.

43.
Develop verbal discipline.

Train your self-talk and your comments to others to focus on the positive, and avoid being judgmental. Instead of stereotyping people into some negative category and labeling them with a derogatory term, look for neutral or positive words. Instead of saying, "This guy will nickel and dime me to death," say "This customer is cost-conscious."

At times you'll have to force yourself to avoid the negative and judgmental, but accept the challenge and you can make a game out of it.

Sincerely try for one full day to avoid saying anything negative or judgmental about another person. If you make it through the day, shoot for another day. Verbal discipline can become a habit that pays off.

You'll find yourself enjoying people more.

44.
Stay current with new business ideas or applications.

Read the business press and keep your eyes open for new ideas. For example, one very hot topic as I write this is indoor air quality. A business that offers janitorial services should probably consider expanding into "interior environment" services. One logical expansion is to offer to pressure vacuum heating and air-conditioning vents to remove buildup of dust, pollens, fungi, etc.

I never knew such businesses existed until I saw a business column write-up describing the health problems and allergies associated with indoor air quality.

Adding a new service or product line provides a great reason to contact your existing customers, too. Let them know what's new via phone, letter or media ads.

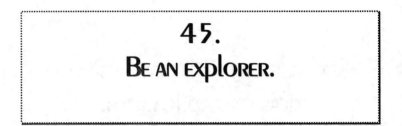

45.
BE AN EXPLORER.

When you hear about a great idea another business is using, send out an exploration party to scope it out.

One supermarket known for exceptional service encourages employees to take a company van and rush to the scene of good service given by others. They take notes and discuss possible implementation in their store.

Other explorer groups can be customers or employees who report their findings to management. Be open to these ideas. Keep your eyes and ears open for new ideas. Sometimes they come from the most unlikely sources.

*Use this space to generate your own ideas on how to **retain** your customers.*

_____

_____

_____

_____

_____

_____

_____

_____

_____

_____

_____

_____

_____

_____

50 Powerful Ways to Win New Customers

*Use this space to generate your own ideas on how to **retain** your customers.*

_____

_____

_____

_____

_____

_____

_____

_____

_____

_____

_____

_____

Use this space to generate your own ideas on how to **retain** *your customers.*

_____

_____

_____

_____

_____

_____

_____

_____

_____

_____

_____

_____

_____

50 Powerful Ways to Win New Customers

Use this space to generate your own ideas on how to ***retain*** *your customers.*

Restore the Lost Customer

Two kinds of actions are needed to restore the lost or potentially lost customer:

1. Recognize and talk to your employees about the terrible cost of lost customers.

2. Apply specific steps to win the unhappy customer back.

46.
BE SURE YOUR EMPLOYEES UNDERSTAND THE COST OF THE LOST CUSTOMER.

Most people don't understand the real cost of a lost customer. When an unhappy customer decides to stop doing business with us, the costs are much more than we realize. I often use the following simple story to illustrate how costly even one lost customer can be. (All names are fictitious. If there is a "Happy Jack's Supermarket" somewhere, it's not the one described in this story.)

Imagine that you are the owner of a grocery supermarket. Mrs. Williams has been shopping at your store, Happy Jack's Supermarket for many years, but who has decided to stop shopping there. She doesn't feel that her business is appreciated.

As you read, try to calculate the cost of these same "ripple effects" on your company.

Good-bye Mrs. Williams

There goes Mrs. Williams. She just checked out her groceries from Happy Jack's Supermarket and she's mad as hell. She's been shopping here for years but the produce man wouldn't even consider making her a smaller package of apples or selling her a half head of lettuce. (He acted like that was the stupidest request he'd ever heard.) The dairy department was out of the quart size skim milk. And then the cashier demanded two forms of identification with her check. What do they think she is, a common criminal?

But worst of all was just an overall feeling that the employees of Happy Jack's could care less if she shopped there. She spends about 50 hard-earned dollars there every week, but to the store employees she's just another cash cow to be milked without so much as a sincere "thank you." Nobody seems to care whether she's a satisfied customer.

But today is different. Mrs. Williams just decided to try shopping elsewhere. Maybe, just maybe, there is a store where they'll appreciate her business.

What do the employees think about that?

They're not worried. Happy Jack's is a pretty big chain and doesn't really need Mrs. Williams. Besides, she can be a bit cranky at times. They'll survive without her $50 a week. Too bad she's unhappy, but a big company like this can't twist itself into contortions just to save one little old lady from going down the street to the competition.

Sure, we believe in treating customers well, but we're businesspeople. Let's look at the bottom line. After all, it can hardly be considered a major financial disaster to lose a few customers like Mrs. Williams. Or can it?

The employees at Happy Jack's need to understand some economic facts of life. Successful businesses look long term. They look at the "ripple effects" of their service, not just at the immediate profit from an individual purchase.

The shortsighted employee sees Mrs. Williams as a small customer dealing with a big company. Let's change that view: look at the situation from another, longer term perspective.

More than the loss of one small customer

The loss of Mrs. Williams is not, of course, a $50 loss. It's much, much more. She was a $50-a-week buyer. That's

$2,600 a year or $26,000 over a decade. Perhaps she would shop at Happy Jack's for a lifetime, but we'll use the more conservative 10-year figure for illustration.

The ripple effects make it much worse. Studies show that *an upset customer tells on average 11 other people about an unhappy experience.* Some people will tell many more, but let's assume that Mrs. Williams told eleven. The same studies say that these 11 *may tell an average of five others each.* This could be getting serious!

How many people are likely to hear the bad news about Happy Jack's? Look at the math:

Mrs. Williams	1
tells eleven others	+11
who tell five each	+55
Total who heard	67

Sure, but all 67 of these people aren't going to rebel against Happy Jack's, are they? Probably not. Let's assume that of these 67 customers or potential customers, only 25 percent decide not to shop at Happy Jack's. Twenty-five percent of 67 (rounded) is 17.

Assuming that these 17 people would also be $50-a-week shoppers, Happy Jack's stands to lose $44,200 a year, or $442,000 in a decade because Mrs. Williams was upset when she left the store.

Although these numbers are starting to get alarming, they are still conservative. A typical supermarket customer actually spends about $100 a week, so losing a different customer could quickly double these figures.

Take a moment and think about how much your customer spends with you. Perhaps he or she buys every month or two or only once every few years. But in almost every case, repeat business is crucial to your success.

Viewing customers as one-time buyers can and will be hazardous to your financial health.

How much will it cost to replace these customers?

Customer service research says that *it costs five to six times as much to attract a new customer* (mostly advertising and promotion costs) *than it does to keep an existing one* (where costs may include giving refunds, offering samples, replacing merchandise). One report put these figures at about $19 to keep a customer happy versus $118 to get a new buyer into the store.

Again, some quick math shows the real cost of the lost Mrs. Williams:

> Cost of keeping Mrs. Williams happy $19
> Cost of attracting 17 new customers $2,006

Now let's make our economic "facts of life" even more meaningful to us.

How the lost customer can mean a lost job

The Robert Half Organization, a well-known personnel consulting firm, shows a simple way to calculate the amount of sales needed to pay employee salaries. Assuming that a company pays 50 percent in taxes and earns a profit of 5 percent after taxes, the chart below shows how much must be sold to pay each employee (in three different salary levels) and maintain current profit levels:

Salary	Benefits	After Tax Cost	Sales Needed
$25,000	$11,500	$18,250	$365,000
$15,000	$ 6,900	$10,950	$219,000
$10,000	$ 4,600	$ 7,300	$146,000

These figures will vary, of course. But the impact on one's job can be clearly shown.

If a $10,000-a-year clerk irritates as few as three or four customers *in a year*, the ripple effects can exceed the amount of sales needed to maintain that job! Unfortunately, many organizations have employees who irritate three or four customers *a day*! Ouch.

Applying Mrs. Williams to your company

What does Mrs. Williams and the grocery store example have to do with you and your business? Basically, the same things can happen. Your unhappy customer will tell other customers or potential customers. They in turn will tell even more people.

Let's take a few moments and go back to the Mrs. Williams example, but instead use your own organization. Supposing you lose one customer and some of the other statistics hold true. Take a few moments to calculate the numbers as they apply to your organization. If you work for a nonprofit or government agency where the dollar sales is not a relevant measure, calculate the number of people who may be aggravated or upset with you and your organization. Think in terms of the psychological price that must be paid as you deal with frustrated, angry, upset patrons on a day-to-day basis.

Help your employees realize in no uncertain terms that a lost customer can be a disaster!

47.
Rebuild a weak reputation.

Suppose you do an organizational reality check (page 18), looking at your company through your customer's eyes, and you don't much like what you see. What now?

Face the situation directly and let people know you are committed to rebuilding your ability to serve customers well. Kmart, the second-largest retailer in the world, has recently dedicated more than $3 billion of its budget to store revitalization, largely in response to the competitive threat of Wal-Mart (now the world's largest retailer).

Here's an example on a smaller scale: The owner of a tire store chain used old-fashioned sincerity to invite customers back to his store. He sent an open letter to his community that apologized for poor service they might have experienced in the past. His letter (modified slightly to protect the guilty) follows.

Really Big Tire Stores
Auto Service Centers
123 Main
Bison Breath, NE

Oct. 1, 1998

An Open Letter to the People of Bison Breath

Some time ago, we discovered that our previous manager and his staff were not taking care of our customers at our Bison Breath store. This is certainly not in keeping with Really Big Tire's guarantee of customer satisfaction, qualified technicians and friendly service. We were extremely disappointed to hear this and we tried to move quickly to correct the situation.

The previous manager was discharged, and on June 27 we transferred Craig Cunningham into the Bison Breath store. Craig is a very competent, courteous manager with years of experience in the tire and automotive industry. Craig, his wife and family are long-term residents of nearby Eastville. Since Craig has been your store manager, we have had many positive comments on his service and dedication to customers' needs.

To show our good faith, and to welcome folks back to our store at 123 Main, we will perform a full lubrication service, change the oil with up to five quarts of Pennzoil oil, install a new oil filter and lube the chassis for only $5.95 upon presentation of this letter at the store.

We are happy to be part of the growing Bison Breath community and will do our best to offer tires and automotive services at the lowest prices in Nebraska with the finest service anywhere.

Sincerely,

T. S. Tim

Tire Store Tim

cc: Honorable James Williams, Mayor
    City of Bison Breath

48.
LISTEN TO THE CUSTOMERS
YOU *didn't* GET.

When people indicate that they bought from a competitor, ask why. Not in an argumentative way, but with sincerity. Simply say that you would have liked to gain their business and ask why they chose another company.

Listen carefully to what they say and you'll get some good tips on how to improve your business.

In every business we can learn from mistakes. It takes courage (and often a thick skin) to ask people what you did wrong. But it can be some of the most useful information you'll ever get.

Remember, the ostrich leaves one end exposed.

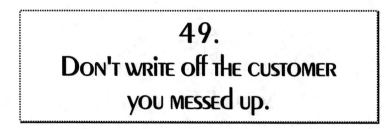

49.
DON'T WRITE OFF THE CUSTOMER YOU MESSED UP.

Okay, so you messed up with customers in the past. They bought something that didn't work or one of your people gave them a hard time. Is all lost? Nope.

It's funny, but true: Customers who have a problem with a company—and the company works hard to fix the problem—actually become more loyal than customers who have never had a problem. Apparently companies and people who develop their "recovery" skills end up with more loyal customers.

Recognize that upset customers want some or all of the following from you:

♦ To be listened to and taken seriously.

♦ That you understand their problem and the reason they are upset.

♦ Compensation or restitution.

♦ A sense of urgency; to get their problem handled quickly.

♦ Avoidance of further inconvenience.

♦ To be treated with respect.

♦ To have someone punished for the problem.

♦ Assurance that the problem will not occur again.

If all goes well, you should feel a genuine sense of satisfaction after handling an unhappy or irate customer. But this is not a perfect world and people are not always rational, so sometimes you, too, get upset. The key things to remember are:

◆ If you try your best to satisfy the customer, you have done all that you can do.

◆ Don't take it personally. Upset people often say things they don't really mean. They are blowing off steam, venting frustration. If the problem was really your fault, resolve to learn from the experience and do better next time. If you had no control over the situation, do what you can, but don't bat your head against the wall.

◆ Don't rehash the experience with your coworkers or in your own mind. What's done is done. Recounting the experience with others probably won't make their day any better, and rehashing it to yourself will just make you mad. You may, however, want to ask another person how they would have handled the situation.

◆ Use every customer contact experience as an opportunity to improve. Even the most unpleasant encounter can teach us useful lessons.

When the situation has cooled, you may want to review with an eye toward improving your skills. Think back on the situation where you used your recovery skills and ask questions like these:

◆ What was the customer's major complaint?

◆ How did the customer see the problem? Who was to blame? What irritated the customer most? Why was he or she angry/frustrated?

- How did you see the problem? Was the customer partially to blame?

- What did you say to the customer that helped the situation?

- What did you say that seemed to aggravate the situation?

- How did you try to show your concern to the customer?

- What would you do differently?

50.
Apologize and make it right.

Some people hate to apologize on behalf of the company, especially when the problem was not one they had direct control over.

Apologizing does not diminish you. It does not need to be an admission of guilt. An apology is an expression of regret that the customer's experience has been less than pleasant.

Giving an apology takes nothing away from you! It expresses the wish that future customer experiences will be more positive. But without an apology, there will be no future customer experiences.

In addition to apologizing, ask customers what you can do to make it right. If their suggestion is anywhere within the realm of possibility, do it.

Then tell others how you fixed the problem.

Part of customer relations is public relations and the first rule of public relations is to *let good deeds be noticed.* If a customer has a problem and you fix it, tell that customer, and, in some cases, tell other customers, too.

Follow-up calls to repair customers to be sure that their problem has been solved (even if you know it has been) reminds them that you care.

For example, an auto service department replaced my car's radio immediately rather than removing it and sending it off for repair. The service manager said he didn't want me to be "driving around with a hole in my dashboard" like other dealerships might have me do—a reminder that he'd given me E-Plus service.

Another time, a bookstore owner called several competitors to see if they had a title I was looking for. Then he called me back to say what he'd done and where I could find it.

These simple gestures not only improve customer service expectations with E-Plus service, but build customer loyalty along the way.

Use this space to generate your own ideas on how to **restore** *your customers.*

_____

_____

_____

_____

_____

_____

_____

_____

_____

_____

_____

_____

_____

_____

50 Powerful Ways to Win New Customers

*Use this space to generate your own ideas on how to **restore** your customers.*

_____

_____

_____

_____

_____

_____

_____

_____

_____

_____

_____

_____

Use this space to generate your own ideas on how to ***restore*** *your customers.*

_____

_____

_____

_____

_____

_____

_____

_____

_____

_____

_____

_____

_____

_____

*Use this space to generate your own ideas on how to **restore** your customers.*

_____

_____

_____

_____

_____

_____

_____

_____

_____

_____

_____

_____

Use this space to generate your own ideas on how to **restore** *your customers.*

_____

_____

_____

_____

_____

_____

_____

_____

_____

_____

_____

_____

_____

Use this space to generate your own ideas on how to **restore** *your customers.*

_____

_____

_____

_____

_____

_____

_____

_____

_____

_____

_____

_____

A Final Few Words

I hope this book stimulates you to sharpen your attitude of inquiry. It really is an attitude, you know. Some people experience thousands of business transactions and never even see what made them work or fail in winning customers. Other people tune in to the process and generate countless ideas they can apply immediately. The determining factor is their attitude of inquiry.

Keep your eyes open. Recognize clever and interesting approaches used by businesses to entice you to buy. Then see which of these might apply to your line of work. You may be surprised at the frequency with which an application can be made.

Getting customers is an art and a science—an art because it calls for creativity and innovation; a science because it call for systematic application of ideas and examination of the results.

Make it your goal—starting today—to apply the customer-getting ideas described in this book as well as others they may trigger in your mind. Try some new behaviors and carefully observe the results. You'll be pleasantly surprised at your success in winning new customers.

> *Whoever acquires knowledge but does not practice it, is as one who ploughs but does not sow.*
>
> —Saadi

About the Author

Dr. Paul R. Timm has written more than 30 books and scores of articles in the fields of customer service, human relations, communication and self-management. He holds a doctorate degree from Florida State University in organizational communication and is chairman of the Department of Management Communication in the Marriott School of Management at Brigham Young University.

As an active consultant and trainer, Timm has worked with thousands of people from organizations throughout North America. He wrote and appears in three videotape training programs sold worldwide including *The Power of Customer Service, Successful Self-Management, and 50 Ways to Keep Your Customers* (available through JWA Televideo, Chicago. Call 312-829-5100 to order.) He is the author of *50 Powerful Ideas You Can Use To Keep Your Customers* (available through Career Press. Call 1-800-CAREER-1 to order.)

For information about Timm's consulting and training services, call 801-378-5682 or fax 801-378-8309.

Index

A

"A" customers, 84
Action categories, 12
Add-ons,
    E-Plus, 78
Advertising,
    consistency, 44
    cross-promoting, 49
    simplicity, 44
Apologizing, to customers,
    109-110
Appearance,
    importance to
        customers, 22
    of workplace, 23
Assuming, sale, 20
AT&T, 24
Attitude, 16, 20
Attract, new customers,
    12-13, 15-54

B

Business cards, 37-38

Business trends, 91
Businesses, failure of, 9

C

Charity, donations
    to, 43, 57
"College Bookstore Invites
    Its Customers to Curl
    Up," 87
Convenience,
    E-Plus, 79-80
Coupon books, 56
Cross-promoting, 49
Customer service, 18-19
Customer-friendly,
    office, 83
Customers
    angry, 106-108
    anticipating needs
        of, 85-86
    apologizing to, 109-110
    attraction of, 12-13,
        15-54

expectations of, 66-68
feeling at home, 87
listening to, 89
lost, 98-102
loyalty of, 106
motivation of, 12-13,
    55-64
points of encounter
    (POEs), 81-82
retention of, 12-13,
    65-96
restoration of, 12-13,
    97-114
satisfaction of, 28-29,
    66-68
teaching, 24-25

D

Discipline, verbal, 90
Display, products, 26
Door-to-door sales, 58
Dun & Bradstreet, 46

E

80/20 Rule, 84
E-mail, 40
E-Plus service, 66-80
    add-ons, 78
    convenience, 79-80
    information, 73
    personality, 75-77
    speed, 74
    value, 71-72

Employees
    hiring, 17
    training, 27
Equity theory, 68-70
EXCHANGE, 74
Expectations, of
    customers, 66-70

F

*50 Powerful Ideas You Can
    Use to Keep Your
    Customers,* 44
Failure, businesses, 9
Fairs, 47-48
Fax machines, 39
Flea markets, 47-48
"Free for All," 78
"From Slogans to Strategy:
    A Workable Approach to
    Customer Satisfaction
    and Loyalty," 74

G

Gallagher, Bill, 36
Girard, Joe, 20, 35
Giveaways, 78
Guerrilla Selling, 36, 38

H

Hiring of employees, 17
*How to Avoid Auto Service
    Ripoffs*, 50

How to Sell Anything to Anybody, 20, 36

I

Information,
E-Plus, 73

K

Kirby vacuum cleaners, 71
Kmart, 103

L

Les Schwab Pride in Performance, 49
Letter campaigns, 59
Levinson, Jay Conrad, 36, 78
Listening, to customers, 89
Lost customers, 98-102
Loyalty, customer, 106

M

MacRae's Blue Book, 46
Marketing
  word of mouth, 32
  network, 32
  multilevel, 36
Multilevel marketing, 36
Million Dollar Directory, 46
Motivate, customers, 12-13, 55-64

N

Needs of customers, anticipating, 85-86
Network marketing, 32

O

Office, customer friendly, 83
Oregon Cattlemen's Association, 49

P

Pagers, 39
Personality, E-Plus, 75-77
Personality, importance to customers, 75-77
POEs, 81-82
Points of encounter (POEs), customers, 81-82
Products
  display of, 26
  showcasing of, 26
Prospect list, building and maintaining, 41
Punch cards, 56

R

R.L. Polk City Directory, 46
Radio, promoting customer satisfaction, 28-29

Referrals, 34
Reputation, rebuilding a
    weak, 103
Restore, customers, 12-13,
    97-114
Retain, customers, 12-13,
    65-96
Ripple effects, 98-100

S

Salespeople, doing away
    with, 88
Salinger, J.D., 21
Satisfaction, customers,
    28-29, 66
Saturn, 88
Schwab, Les, 49
Service, customer, 18-19
Showcasing, products, 26
Slogans, 18
Speed,
    E-Plus, 74
Success, broadcasting, 45

T

Teaching, customers, 24-25
Technology, advantage
    of, 39-40
Telephone, techniques, 30-31

Toll-free numbers, 39
Toyota, 79
Trade shows, 47-48
    pre-invitations, 47
    giveaways, 47
    working at, 48
    follow up, 48
Training of employees, 27
Trends, business, 91

V

Value,
    E-Plus, 71-72
Verbal discipline, 90

W

Wal-Mart, 103
*Wall Street Journal,
    The*, 87
Web pages, 40
Western Auto freezers, 71
Wilson, Orvil Ray, 36
Winning Telephone Tips, 31
Word of mouth
    marketing, 32

Y

Yellow pages, listing in, 46